DOCTOR GENIUS
AND
THE MAD SCIENTISTS

THE FLASK
OF DOOM

Clive Gifford

Designed by Russell Punter
Illustrated by Geo Parkin

Series Editor: Jane Chisholm

CONTENTS

MEET THE MAD SCIENTISTS

The Mad Scientists are a team of great brains and little common sense. They are dedicated to using science for good to make the world a better, safer place. The intrepid leader of this amazing gang is Dr. Genius.

In their rambling collection of laboratories and workshops, the Mad Scientists are constantly tinkering away with new ideas and inventions. But they rarely finish them off. Why? For three important reasons.

One: they're not interested in becoming rich. Provided they have enough money to buy the occasional piece of new equipment, then they're happy.

Two: they're too scatterbrained to follow a project through.

Three: the most important reason of all, they're far too busy solving mysteries, uncovering dastardly plots and overcoming evil superbrains, to finish their own scientific work.

To the Mad Scientists, the most important task is to stop criminal masterminds from using science for their own evil ends.

Each member of the team is particularly clever in one area of science and fairly stupid when it comes to other areas! For example, brilliant biologist, Rosie Bloom, wouldn't know one end of a car from the other, while expert physicist, Frank Quark, probably couldn't tell a cat and a kangaroo apart.

MAD SCIENTISTS

Name: Dr. GENIUS

Job: Leader

Interests: Saving the world from super villains
Collecting antiques
Sleeping in late

MAD SCIENTISTS

Name: ROSIE BLOOM

Job: Biologist

Interests: Her pet mouse, Einstein
Hiking
Bird-watching
Gardening

MAD SCIENTISTS

Name: FRANK QUARK

Job: Physicist

Interests: Fast cars
Reading
Playing Chess
Winning bets

MAD SCIENTISTS

Name: SUKI BEAKER

Job: Chemist

Interests: Crosswords
Cooking
Mountain biking

MAD SCIENTISTS

Name: ELTON BOLT

Job: Engineer

Interests: Dragster racing
Fishing
Playing the guitar

MAD SCIENTISTS

Name: KEN PLANK

Job: Lab Assistant

Interests: Computers
Astronomy
Sports and games

As you read the adventures of Dr. Genius and his team, you will come across puzzles and scientific problems that are there for you to solve. If you get stuck, you can turn to the answers starting at page 44.

3

One sunny morning, the Mad Scientists were all huddled around some apparatus in their labs. Two tennis balls dangled from strings. Suki rushed in.

"Dr. Genius! I've something important to tell you."
"Not now Suki," said Dr. Genius, "Frank has a bet on with Elton." Suki went quiet.

"I bet you can't get those tennis balls to touch without you touching them, the table or the apparatus," said Frank.
"Impossible," Rosie gasped.
"Easy," grinned Elton confidently.

"Watch out for that lump of Boomtex," warned Dr. Genius.
"What's Boomtex?" asked Ken.
"It's a new, highly dangerous explosive which goes off whenever it touches water. I'm doing some tests on a sample for the Blue Carnation Club," explained Suki.

"What sort of club is that?" asked Ken.
"It's only for the very best scientists, dedicated to cleaning up the planet," replied Suki. "The famous explosives expert, Dr. Grossenbang, is lecturing there soon, explaining why Boomtex should be banned."

Elton took a deep breath and blew as hard as possible between the tennis balls, which came together and touched.

"Blowing the air creates lower air pressure which helps to force the balls together," lectured Elton smugly. Frank started to throw a temper tantrum.

Distracted by Frank's outburst, it took a while for anyone to notice the ball of Boomtex rolling along the desk. Suki saw it first and cried, "It's going to touch water!"

"You don't have to worry," replied Ken casually. "The sink's on the other side of the room."

Can you see what Suki thinks will make the Boomtex explode?

5

SLICK'S STORY

As the smoke cleared, six black faces stared at each other in surprise. "The Boomtex fell into a bucket marked H_2O, the symbol for water," explained Suki with a sigh.

The scientists cleaned themselves up while Suki explained why she had rushed in. "You remember I gave Slickspin Labs my notes on how to make an antifriction liquid? Well, Professor Slick, who's in charge of the labs, has actually managed to make a flask of the stuff. A little of it diluted - that's mixed with water for those who don't know - makes a really incredible low friction paint."

"Sounds like a marvellous advance, Suki, so why are you upset?" asked Dr. Genius. "Because the only flask of the liquid that exists has just been stolen," replied Suki.

Dr. Genius turned to Frank, "Call Professor Slick and tell her we'll be over in a flash."

The Mad Scientists hurried over to Slickspin Labs but Simone Slick was nowhere to be seen. She had left a note, however.

> I WILL BE LATE. HAVE LOST SOME OF MY KEYS. WAIT IN MY MAIN OFFICE.
>
> SIMONE SLICK

As the Scientists entered Slick's plush office, Elton spotted a photo and said, "Look, it's Frank's dream car, the Fandango Seven." "That's what Simone Slick wants as well. She's been on the waiting list for ten years," explained Suki.

Yes, and I've still got fifteen more years to wait. Sorry I'm late. I've been looking for my keys. I had to use one of the spares I keep hidden under the tall lamp in my study.

"Frank said you might be able to help," Slick said, scanning the Scientists' faces doubtfully. "First, you'll need to know all about friction. It's the resistance caused by two things rubbing against each other. It causes wear and slows things down. When you oil the wheels of your bike, you are reducing friction so the wheels run more smoothly." "We know," said Elton testily. "I didn't," disagreed Rosie, "please continue, Simone." "It's Professor Slick to you," Slick snapped back.

"To continue, the point is my liquid cuts down friction to almost nothing," boasted Slick.

"It could have many useful applications. I was planning to build outdoor skating rinks in hot countries. The antifriction liquid would replace the ice and not melt in the hot sun. I've had lots of interest from...oh, what's that country called? You know, the one from where those animals come," she said, pointing to some postcards pinned to the wall.

Can you guess which country Simone Slick is talking about?

SLIP UP STICK UP

Not far away, a robbery was taking place as Professor Slick talked. A sinister figure in a silk robe was robbing the local bank. He held a very strange pistol, while his two tough henchmen looked on.

The Bank Manager and his senior clerk dragged two heavy sacks of money from the safe. "If I can ask just one more thing," the strange man said with a sneer. "Please hold your noses as my associates come around."

The intruder's two henchmen started dabbing the hands and feet of the staff and customers with a stinking green liquid.

The smell was terrible, like a cross between old socks and boiled cabbage. Even the telephones received a coating.

The last drops of the liquid were used on a customer's dog before the two tough men grabbed the bulging, brown sacks.

The man with the gun turned to the startled onlookers and said, "I am Max Chaos, and these are my two associates, Bother and Trouble. The 5400 seconds of fun you're about to have are supplied courtesy of the Flask of Doom. We thank you!"

And with that, he pointed the pistol at the security guard and pulled the trigger. "So long," he said with a smile.

Chuckling to themselves, the three troublemakers strolled casually out of the bank. The bank clerk immediately tried to grab the security phone, but it kept slipping out of his hand. "It's the paint," he cried as he fell.

Panic set in as everyone tumbled over, unable to get up. By the time the police arrived, Max Chaos and his men were far away.

What time will it be when the paint's effects wear off?

9

THE FAX OF FEAR

B ack at Slickspin Labs, Simone Slick was still lecturing the others.

"It's not Indian orders I'm worried about, it's what the liquid could do in the wrong hands."

"What do you mean?" asked Ken.

"Well, we often need friction," Slick replied.

"For what?" enquired Rosie.

"For walking, standing up, holding things. Friction provides us with the grip to do all this and a lot, lot more," Slick explained.

"Friction is what makes brakes work. Think of a car without brakes." Ken and the others shuddered in horror. "Now you see why I'm so worried," snapped Slick impatiently.

Meanwhile, Ken was absorbed by a photo on the wall.

"Air passing over an object creates friction too," interrupted Slick. "That's how the parachute on that jet plane works. The parachute increases friction which slows the plane down."

"Oh, I see," said Elton, "It's like the parachute I sometimes use on my racing dragster."

"Of course, there'll be a reward if the flask is recovered," said Slick. "Oh we're not interested in money," replied Rosie. "We just don't want to see the liquid used for evil purposes."

"I must work on a friction restorer, so push off," Slick interrupted, quickly opening the door.

"How rude," muttered Elton.

"I'll show her," said Suki.

The next day, back at their labs, Suki was also working on her own friction restorer. "I'm going to beat Simone Slick and make it first," she declared.

"I don't mind who wins just as long as one of you makes a friction restorer and fast," muttered Dr. Genius, frowning over the newspaper reports.

THE NEWS HERALD

CRIMINAL CHAOS COPS CASH !

Chaos, captured on film by security cameras.

Slickspin Labs' stolen anti-friction liquid was used by supercriminal Max Chaos as he made off with a huge stack of cash. Although by 1pm the liquid's effects had worn off, most of the victims are still in St Mary's Hospital, recovering from shock and bruises. Prof. Simone Slick, head of the Labs, is reported to be working day and night on a friction restorer which will act as an antidote to the liquid contained in what Max Chaos has nicknamed, 'The Flask of Doom'.

GLOVES GOES

Top of the table Albion Rovers are still in shock after their 21-0 loss last night at the hands of relegation candidates, No Hopes Utd. Blame for the record defeat has been firmly placed in the slippery hands of top international goalie, Gordon Gloves, who was fired last night after finding it impossible to hold onto the ball throughout the match. But the amazing scoreline has netted one mystery figure a fortune when he or she placed a 50,000-1 bet on Rovers to lose by more than 15 goals.

Gloves- "I can't understand it."

SSL ✳

FRICTION
RESTORER
FINISHED
INTRUDERS
ABOUT TO
DISCOVER ME
HAVE LEFT IN A
HELP

Later that night, a garbled message came through on the Scientists' fax machine. "It looks like whole lines of dots on Slick's dot matrix printer aren't working," said Frank. "Nice to see something of Slick's not working," sniggered Elton. "Shh. Let's try to work the message out," urged Suki.

"Oh dear," sighed Dr. Genius, as he deciphered the message. "Suki, stay here and work on your friction restorer," he said. "The rest of us must get over to Slickspin Labs without delay."

Can you work out what Prof. Slick's message says?

PLANT PUZZLE

The Scientists entered Slickspin Labs on the stroke of midnight. Walking up a flight of stairs, they reached a long, sloping hallway. "Let's head for Simone Slick's office," said Dr. Genius, cautiously scanning the corridor for signs of danger.
"What's that funny smell?" asked Rosie, her nose in the air.
"I don't know, but be on guard," replied Elton, trembling nervously.
"Calm down," smiled Frank, "there's nothing to fear....ARGH!"

The Scientists slipped and slid along the sloping hallway. They tumbled down some stairs and crashed into a large room. Behind them the door slammed shut and they could hear the muffled sound of two deep voices laughing. They realized they were in Professor Slick's study.

The study had been ransacked. "What a mess!" exclaimed Ken. "I bet Chaos was behind this," sighed Frank, hands on hips.

Elton picked up the lamp from the floor and plugged it in. "How are we ever going to get out, Doc?" he asked wearily.

"Well, Slick did say something about spare keys hidden underneath the lamp," replied Dr. Genius brightly.

"But we don't know where the lamp first stood," moaned Frank. "You may not, but the plants do!" cried Rosie triumphantly. "She's gone bonkers!" wailed Ken. "No," corrected Dr. Genius, "I think Rosie has the answer."

How does Rosie know?

13

A KEY NOTE

Rosie dropped to her knees in the corner between the plants. "The keys should be under here," she said through gritted teeth, as she ripped up a carpet tile. "Here they are!" It didn't take Rosie long to select the correct key and unlock the door.

"Well done!" cheered Ken. "How did you know that, a youngster like you?" huffed Frank rudely.
"Plants grow towards light. You should have done more biology at school, Frank," teased Rosie.
"Now, now. Let's stop the arguing and start searching for clues instead," interrupted Dr. Genius. "Oh and bring those strips of litmus paper, Frank. They could be useful later."

As Frank grabbed the litmus paper, Elton picked up a strange scrap from a notebook that had been lying on the floor. He started studying it as the Mad Scientists tiptoed down the hallway and into a high-tech laboratory.

"So this is what you get when you sell your inventions," said Frank enviously.

"Come on now, Frank," said Dr. Genius, "We care about science more than money, don't we?"

"Yes, you're right," said Frank. "And anyway, you've got more chance of moving to the top of the waiting list for a Fandango Seven car than selling your silly ideas," laughed Ken.

Rosie left Frank and Ken to their arguing and turned to Elton. "Have you seen the tool cupboard?" she asked. But Elton was still thinking about the piece of paper he had picked up from Simone Slick's study.

"I think this piece of paper contains a clue," he declared.

What does the piece of paper tell the Mad Scientists?

CODED CHEMICALS

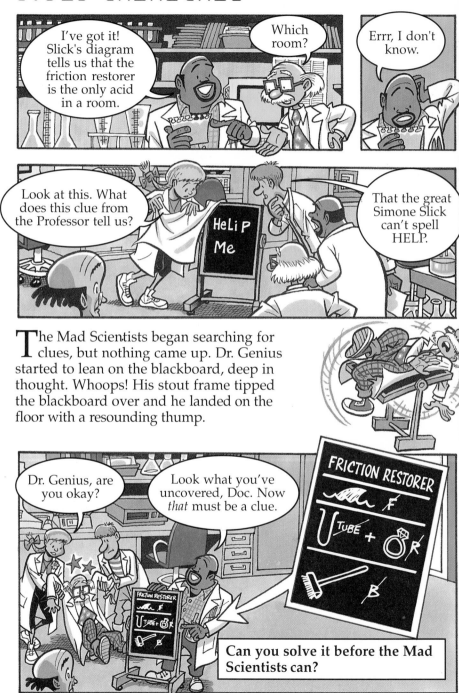

I've got it! Slick's diagram tells us that the friction restorer is the only acid in a room.

Which room?

Errr, I don't know.

Look at this. What does this clue from the Professor tell us?

HeLiP Me

That the great Simone Slick can't spell HELP.

The Mad Scientists began searching for clues, but nothing came up. Dr. Genius started to lean on the blackboard, deep in thought. Whoops! His stout frame tipped the blackboard over and he landed on the floor with a resounding thump.

Dr. Genius, are you okay?

Look what you've uncovered, Doc. Now *that* must be a clue.

FRICTION RESTORER

U TUBE + R

B

Can you solve it before the Mad Scientists can?

The door to the testing room was locked fast. There was no lock or handle, only an unusual electronic pad by the door. The code pad had the names of lots of chemical elements.
"Which buttons do we press?" wondered Elton.
"And in what order?" added Ken.

"Of course, the other side of the blackboard," cried Frank loudly. He started pushing buttons on the keypad and muttered, "Clever Simone Slick and her clues." Amazingly, the door opened smoothly.
"How did he do that?" mumbled a bewildered Elton, as Frank smugly led the Scientists into the testing room.

Which keys do you think Frank pressed to open the door?

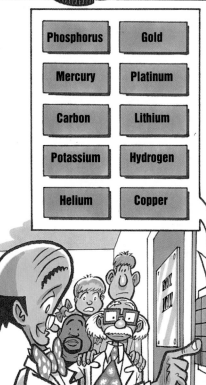

Phosphorus	Gold
Mercury	Platinum
Carbon	Lithium
Potassium	Hydrogen
Helium	Copper

FLASK TASK

The Mad Scientists stared aghast. Row upon row of flasks filled the testing room. Shocked Frank dropped one of the pieces of litmus paper by mistake and groaned. "It's an impossible task," sighed Elton. "Not necessarily," said Dr. Genius. "We have litmus paper and the antidote is the only *acid* in the room, remember?"

It's all about knowing your chemical symbols. Now let's just test these flasks...

18

Suddenly, a loud bang made the Scientists jump.
"What was that?" asked Rosie.
"It sounded suspiciously like someone slamming the door," replied Dr. Genius.

Out of the corner of his eye, Ken spotted one of the flasks, disturbed by the slammed door, teetering on the edge of the shelf. As it hurtled down, he made a heroic dive to catch it.

Good catch, Ken!

But, as Ken took a victory bow, he bumped another flask off the shelves. This one hit the floor with a resounding crash.
"Sorry. One less to test, I suppose," mumbled Ken, trying to avoid the sharp stares and letting liquid from the flask he had caught drip onto the floor.
"What a buffoon!" exclaimed Elton.

"Not at all," said Dr. Genius. "In fact, I think Ken has saved us all a lot of time."

How has Ken solved the flask task?

19

ALL TIED UP

"See, the litmus paper has turned pink where the flask dripped onto it. It's an acid."

"Look, its formula is written on a label."

"We have the friction restorer, excellent!"

"Yes, well done Ken."

"Max Chaos!"

"How observant. Now hand me that friction restorer or the boys here will make you."

"With this friction restorer destroyed and with its maker, Simone Slick, tied up, you are powerless to stop me."

As the truck raced to his secret hideout, Chaos began lecturing the Scientists. "Robbing banks, fixing soccer matches and kidnapping is just a start, you know," he sneered. "A start?" queried Frank. "Yes, on my path to world domination," Chaos replied. "And how are you going to manage that?" Ken sneered back.

"Listen, Kid," said Chaos getting angry, "I've got evil plans and inventions which only the cream of the world's scientists could stop. So, getting rid of all those do-gooding top brains will leave the way clear for me. And, I can't think of a better group to do away with first than that eco-friendly bunch of spoilsports, the Blue Carnation Club."

"But the members of the Blue Carnation Club have been responsible for many of the things that make the world a better place," protested Rosie.

"Precisely," declared Chaos. "That's why they've got to go. You see, I'm looking forward to a world with no silly safety rules and no stupid bans on weapons or dangerous chemicals, a world in which I will be leader."
"But you'll ruin Earth," cried Frank despairingly.
"Yes, eventually I might, but not before I've had a great time," Chaos roared with laughter.
"He's mad," whispered Elton.

"Whatever your exact plan is Chaos, you'll never get away with it," declared Rosie.
"Oh, I think I will. After all, with you trapped in my secret lair, who's going to stop me?"
"These ropes won't hold us for long," said Ken bravely.
"No, but in my factory, I've a cage and an electricity-powered magnet on a crane which will," replied Chaos.

"Don't worry," whispered Rosie, "I've held onto something which may foil his plans."

Do you know what Rosie has kept which may help?

THE CAGE OF CHAOS

When the blindfolds were taken off, the tied-up Scientists gasped in horror. They were in the middle of the worst-looking factory in the world. Above them was a steel cage held on the end of a crane operated by one of Chaos's thugs.

"Welcome to my Kingdom," declared Max Chaos.
"It's awful," moaned Elton, "leaking boilers, bad pipes, fire hazards everywhere."
"And the pollution. It's a nightmare," added Rosie, shuddering.
"Thank you. I do try," smirked Max Chaos. He wandered over to some wiring and pulled two connectors apart. With a loud clang, the cage dropped around the Mad Scientists.

"I'd hoped to fit a proper switch to this crane," Chaos explained, "but I hadn't expected to catch you all so soon. And now, if you'll excuse me I'm off to have an explosive time."

"Chaos has won," moaned Ken.
"Not if we can get those two wires to touch," said Elton. "They'll switch on the magnet and lift this cage."
"But we can't reach," wailed Frank.
"I **bet** you can," said Dr. Genius mysteriously.

EXTREMELY TOXIC

How do you think the two electromagnet wires can be joined?

23

OUT OF THE FRYING PAN...

Rosie frowned. "None of us can reach those wires though." "Bets...bets? Of course! The bet with Elton," laughed Frank loudly and, with that, he blew as hard as he could between the wires. The connectors came together and suddenly, the magnet on the crane came to life and picked up the cage.

"Quick, now!" Dr. Genius cried and the Mad Scientists hopped off the platform. They landed in a heap on the floor just before the wires came apart, switched the magnet off and sent the cage crashing down.

"What about this rope?" asked Ken.
"Um...er...I've just remembered," blushed Elton, "I had a knife in my tool belt all along." After a few moments of fumbling, the Mad Scientists were free.

"You see," boasted Frank, "if I hadn't known about air pressure, and demonstrated it earlier with those tennis balls, we'd never have escaped."

"No time to stand here congratulating yourself Frank," said Dr. Genius. "From what Max Chaos said in the truck, I think he's planning to strike at Dr. Grossenbang's lecture at the Blue Carnation Club tomorrow. We haven't much time."

"No, and we're in real trouble," hissed Ken. "Look behind you. That fire's between us and the only way out."

"Fire needs three things: heat, fuel and air, and it's certainly got plenty of all three," noted Rosie. "But we've no water to put it out," cried Frank. Elton said nothing, but just started taking off his lab coat.
"Don't waste time Elton," squealed Rosie impatiently. "We're in real trouble."

What do you think Elton is going to do with his coat?

25

NO WAY OUT?

Elton flung his coat on the fire and then insisted that Rosie take her coat off too, which he threw onto the flames.

Ignoring Rosie's cries, Frank and Ken added their coats and Elton started stamping feverishly on top of them all.

The coats were quickly reduced to a black, charred mess as the fire died down. "Phew, what a relief," sighed Ken.

"Fire needs heat to start it and fuel and oxygen to keep it going," said Elton with a self-satisfied grin. "By smothering the fire with our coats, I took away one of the three things fire needs: oxygen in the air."

"But you also took my jacket," Rosie moaned, still very upset. "Don't worry, we've plenty of spares at home," soothed Frank. "Yes, but mine had a very special label in its pocket. The label had the formula of the friction restorer written on it," she cried. "Oh, sorry," mumbled Elton.

"Chaos must already have destroyed Slick's friction restorer," said Dr. Genius. "So, let's get back and see if our chemist, Suki, has made her own version."

The Scientists climbed the stairs into another part of the factory, but suddenly stopped in horror.

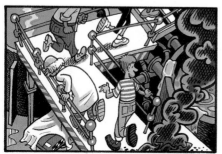

"Look!" said Ken. "That sneak Chaos and his cronies have covered most of the paths with the low friction paint. If we slip, we'll fall."

Can you spot a safe route out of the factory?

DILUTION SOLUTION

Back at their base, Elton phoned the police about Simone Slick's kidnapping. The others watched Suki as she completed her friction restorer. All except Dr. Genius, who rummaged around his messy cupboard pulling out the strangest things.

Suki leaned back and put her hand on her hip, "Great, my own formula friction restorer is finished. All it now needs is some pure water to dilute it with," she announced.

"Easy," said Rosie, "you have a big vat full of it over there."

"Well it was full until the boys started having water fights last week," scowled Suki.

The three men all bowed their heads. "What, you as well, Dr. Genius?" gasped Rosie in astonishment.
"Well, it seemed like harmless fun at the time," he replied with a sneaky grin.

"Look, I've got to go, I'll see you at the Blue Carnation Club," said Dr. Genius, carrying a large suitcase with what looked like a snorkel sticking out of the side. "But Dr. Genius..." But Dr. Genius had gone.

"He's not off to a tropical island is he?" muttered Ken.

"No," said Frank, "I'm sure he's got some amazing plan up his lab coat sleeve."

Dr. Genius popped his head back around the door.

"Oh, by the way, we're at sea level here. So, to get your pure water Suki, stick a thermometer in each of those samples and boil them," he said, before shutting the door and disappearing again. "Of course," cried Suki. The others stared at her, puzzled.

How will the thermometers find the pure water sample?

THE BLUE CARNATION CLUB

Suki chose the water that boiled at exactly 100°C and mixed it with the friction restorer in the two spray bottles. The Scientists rushed to the Blue Carnation Club, where a burly doorman refused them entry. "You scientists thought of everything," grumbled Ken, "...except how to get in."

In the gardens of the club, Dr. Grossenbang had already started his lecture, but some of the distinguished scientists in the audience were getting restless.

Is it me, or is the lake moving closer to Dr. Grossenbang?

I think it's the doctor moving to the lake, actually. Gulp!

Help!

Watch Out!

$$(E_{n+}ME) \Rightarrow \lambda z\lambda$$

BOOMTEX

THE GROSSENBANG LECTURE

PUMP

In the distance, huffing and puffing, Trouble and Bother were pulling on strong ropes.

Phew! I see Max Chaos isn't around for the real work.

Well at least that liquid stuff he put on the grass makes the pulling easier.

Meanwhile, outside the club, Rosie had surprised the others.

Real carnations aren't blue. Painted it in a couple of minutes, eh?

No, I used some ink and waited overnight.

Why so long?

What was Rosie waiting for?

FLOWER POWER

They're with me.

Rosie explained how she left the flower's stem in blue ink overnight and how it drew the ink up into its petals.
"Wow, magic!" Elton exclaimed.
"Not magic, capillary action," corrected Rosie. "Haven't you seen my poster in our labs?"

Displaying the blue carnation, Rosie led the others into the club. A waiter escorted them into the garden. Immediately, they spotted Chaos's helpers pulling the platform towards the lake.

"If that Boomtex lands in the lake, there's going to be a very big explosion," warned Suki.

"The grass behind the platform must have been painted with the antifriction liquid," added Frank.

Frank and Suki rushed over with the friction restorer and sprayed the grass just behind the platform. The wooden stand holding the Boomtex came to a standstill. Try as they might, Trouble and Bother couldn't pull it any further.
"Bloomin' Chaos's plan has gone wrong," said Bother.
"Quick, let's get out of here," replied Trouble.

From behind a statue Max Chaos appeared looking very angry. He grabbed a water pump and hose lying nearby. "Fools! Did you really think you could stop me?" he shouted.

"I don't need that stupid antifriction liquid anymore," he screamed, pulling the near-empty Flask of Doom out of the pocket of his long silk gown and tossing it into the lake.

"If I can't get the Boomtex into the lake, I'll get some of the lake onto the Boomtex," Max Chaos sneered, as he threw the hose into the water. Max Chaos started to back away from the onlookers who all became aware of his terrible plan and started to scream, shout and panic.

"Keep calm folks," urged the waiter in hushed tones.

Where have you seen the waiter before?

THE DIVING SAVE

Everyone went silent. No one dared move. Max Chaos scanned all the frightened faces in front of him and laughed. "You do-gooding meddlers are all doomed, DOOMED!" he roared.

But Chaos didn't see a pair of hands slowly appear from out of the lake...

Max Chaos stepped back, keeping the lump of Boomtex in the sight of his jet-powered hose. Suddenly, he slipped and fell. He fired the hose, just before he tumbled into the lake, but a strong blast of nothing more than air came out. It knocked the Boomtex off its stand and sent it soaring into the air.

THE GROSSENBANG LECTURE

"Catch it!" everyone yelled. Elton and Ken jumped for it but crashed into each other. As they fell to the ground, they collided with Rosie, who was about to grab it with her butterfly net.

Suki screamed, "Watch out!" Suddenly, with an athletic leap, the waiter made a spectacular dive. He caught the Boomtex and held it up to loud cheers from all the scientists.

In the excitement, everyone was too busy congratulating the waiter to notice the two people in the water. One clambered out of the far side of the lake and ran off into the distance. The other watched for a moment.

Then he tried to pull himself out of the lake.

Who is this second figure?

PROBLEM SOLVED?

S uki was the first to recognize him. "Look, it's Dr. Genius!" she cried. The Scientists all helped him out of the water. "What a drip," joked Elton. The others all looked at Elton and groaned.

"But you saved the Blue Carnation Club," roared Dr. Grossenbang, "Congratulations!"

"I think Gordon Gloves here did as much as me," said Dr. Genius, smiling at the tall man. "Oh, it was nothing," Gordon replied.

"Well, Gordon, I'd better speak to your manager," said Dr. Genius, "I think the reason you let in lots of goals was that Max Chaos painted your gloves with antifriction fluid."

"Now, we have the antifriction flask," said Suki in triumph. "But it's empty and Max Chaos has escaped," moaned Ken. "Yes, I'm still worried about him," mumbled Dr. Genius. "But there's nothing we can do at the moment so let's get back to our labs," he sniffed. "Three hours in a freezing lake is enough for ... achhooo ... anyone ... achooo!" "Oh dear, let's get Dr. Genius home to dry out," soothed Rosie.

Dr. Genius wandered into the labs late the next morning. Only Elton was around, tinkering with his dragster.

"Where are the others?" Dr. Genius asked.

"Oh, Rosie's taken her mouse to the vet and the others have gone for a drive in Slick's new car."

"You didn't want to go?" asked Dr. Genius.

"No, she was showing off," replied Elton, "And anyway, my dragster's much faster than her new Fandango Seven."

"But I thought she had another 15 years to wait to get one of those?" Dr. Genius frowned.

"She did, but some anonymous person sold her his almost-new model," Elton replied.

"What did it look like?"

"Racing Red."

"With a black and white stripe down the side?"

Elton nodded.

"Oh dear. Do you know where they were heading?"

"The coastal road to the Macadam Cliffs, I think."

"Oh double dear! Is your dragster working, Elton?"

"Yes, I was just fixing the parachute pack in."

"Don't bother, give me the pack and let's get after them."

"What's the problem, Doc?" asked Elton, as the dragster raced away from the labs.

"I think I've seen the car before and if I'm right, its brakes won't be working, which means they're all in terrible danger."

Where did Dr. Genius see the car before, and what's stopped the brakes from working?

END OF THE ROAD

Simone Slick's new car raced onto the coast road. Frank had been in a trance since the journey's start. He just muttered strange statistics, while Professor Slick demonstrated her fast driving skills.

Fandango Seven. Top speed 261km/h (180mph), 0-100km/h in 3.24 seconds, V12 engine delivering 496bhp at its top end...

Frank certainly knows his cars.

No, just this car. He's got photos of it all over his part of the labs.

Simone Slick rounded a sharp corner just avoiding a crash. "Careful!" shouted Suki.
"I can't help it, the brakes aren't working," Slick screamed back.
"Turn the car around," pleaded Ken, starting to sweat.
"It's too fast to control. We'll crash if I try that," replied Slick, wrestling with the wheel.
Panic broke out.

Simone Slick tried to slow the car down by driving back and forth across the road, but the cliffs were almost in view.

Behind, in the dragster, Elton had raced along all the shortcuts he knew and was catching up with the red Fandango Seven.

As the chase continued, Dr. Genius explained his theory. "I spotted a red car under some covers at Chaos's factory. It matches your description. I think Chaos must have secretly sold the car to Simone Slick."

"Oh no!" exclaimed Elton. "Oh yes," said Dr. Genius. "And what's worse, I reckon that Max Chaos coated the brakes of the car with the antifriction liquid. So hurry up Elton, we must catch them."

Spurred on by the terrible news, Elton raced his dragster alongside Professor Slick's car. Dr. Genius threw the parachute pack to Ken who immediately realized what to do. He grabbed the pack and started tying it to the frame of the car. Elton slammed on the brakes of his dragster and shouted, "Come on Ken! You can do it." Ken didn't let them down. He pulled the ripcord with all his might and the parachute opened out behind the car.

What is the parachute going to do?

MAKE OR BRAKE

Dr. Genius started to explain. "Your dragster parachute will create lots of air friction which will slow the car down." "But will it do it in time, Doc?" asked a very worried Elton.

The fall never came. When all four managed to pull their hands from their faces, they relaxed. "Phew! We made it," sighed Slick. "Let's get out of here," said Frank opening the door. "Whoooahh, there's no ground below me!" The car was balancing on the edge of the cliff.

"Don't move!" bellowed Dr. Genius. "Simone Slick and Frank must go first. Climb into the back of the car and then out onto the cliff."
"But Dr. Genius, what about us?" cried Suki.
"Your turn will come. Just do as I say," Dr. Genius urged.

Nearby, a familiar figure was watching.

They may have overcome the last of the antifriction liquid I put on the brakes...But they're still in big trouble.

Why has Dr Genius insisted on Frank and Simone getting out of the car first?

41

CLIFFHANGER

Frank and Professor Slick scrambled out of the car then Dr. Genius allowed Ken and Suki to climb to safety too.

"That was mean, Dr. Genius," said Suki sniffing a little. "I assure you it wasn't," replied Dr. Genius. "You see, the car was perched on the cliffs' edge and was acting like a balance. If the people in the back had got out first, the weight would have been more in the front and Simone Slick's car would have toppled over the cliffs."

"You saved us!" Ken cried. "Well, it was all to do with the laws of physics really," Dr. Genius shrugged modestly.

"Yes, well done," mumbled Simone Slick impatiently. "Now, you lot can help pull my car back onto the road."

Just as the Mad Scientists finished dragging Professor Slick's Fandango Seven back to safety, a cyclist pulled up.

Gordon Gloves jumped off his bike and greeted the Mad Scientists. "I've been looking for you so that I could say thanks. Now my boss knows my gloves were covered with antifriction liquid, I've got my goalkeeping job back. And what's more, I've been picked for the World Cup squad," Gordon said proudly. He handed the delighted Scientists some free match tickets before hopping back on his training bike.

Seething with rage, the familiar figure slammed his binoculars to the floor and threw an enormous tantrum. "Those blasted Mad Scientists," he screamed. "First they stopped me from blowing up the Blue Carnation Club, then my factory was raided by police and now I've used up the last of the Flask of Doom. I'm finished. Boo Hoo!" One of the figure's henchmen picked up the binoculars and comforted him. "There, there, Mr. Chaos, Sir. It's just a temporary setback."

"Maybe, you're right, Bother," sniffed Max Chaos, starting to cheer up. "I'll be back, I'll get rid of all those scientists and then world power will be mine, all mine, as long as I'm Max Chaos, Criminal Superbrain."

DR. GENIUS EXPLAINS...

Pages 4-5
The Boomtex explosive is triggered off by water. Suki is worried because she sees the explosive rolling off the table toward a bucket marked H_2O, the chemical formula for water.

All substances are made up of tiny particles called atoms. There are over 100 different types of atoms, called elements, each with its own shortened name, called a chemical symbol. A chemical formula tells scientists precisely what elements a substance contains.

Atoms joined together with other atoms are called molecules. A water molecule is made up of two hydrogen atoms and one oxygen atom. Scientists write this as H_2O.

Pages 6-7
The country that Professor Slick is referring to is India. All three animals shown on the postcards come from there. The animals are the Bengal Tiger, the Indian Elephant and the King Cobra snake. The Indian elephant has much smaller ears than the African elephant.

Pages 8-9
The antifriction liquid will stop working at 1 o'clock. The bank's digital clock says 11:30 when Max Chaos paints the antifriction liquid onto the people in the bank. Max Chaos says the liquid's effects will last for 5400 seconds. There are 3600 seconds in an hour (60 seconds x 60 minutes) so 5400 seconds is an hour and a half.

Pages 10-11
Slick's message should read:

FRICTION RESTORER FINISHED. INTRUDERS ABOUT TO KIDNAP ME. HAVE LEFT CLUES. HELP!

A dot matrix printer uses rows and rows of steel pins to strike an ink ribbon, leaving a pattern of dots on the paper. The dots form a letter or number. The column of pins on the extreme left of Slick's printer isn't working. That is why parts of the letters are missing in her note.

Pages 12-13
Rosie knows where the lamp stood because she spotted that all the plants in the study are bending toward the same place.

All plants need light as well as water to grow. Plant stems and leaves bend toward the light. This is called phototropism.

The plants in Slick's study all bend to the same place. Rosie works out that there must have been a source of light there before, such as the tall lamp.

Pages 14-15

The clue on the note tells Elton that there is only one flask in the room that contains an acid. The clue is in the form of a Venn diagram. Venn diagrams show items in and out of sets and the relationship between two sets. The first circle is the set showing acids. Lemons, vinegar and the acid in batteries are all acids.

The second circle is the set showing what's in the room. 1000 flasks are in the room. Venn diagrams also show the relationships between sets. If something is in the area made by two sets overlapping, it can fit in either set. Only one flask is both in the room and in the acid set.

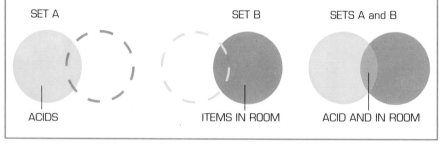

SET A — ACIDS

SET B — ITEMS IN ROOM

SETS A and B — ACID AND IN ROOM

Page 16

Professor Slick's message is: *friction restorer in testing room.*

The clue she left was a simple word and picture puzzle. A

shark's fin without the *f* equals **in**. A test tube without the *tube* and a ring without the *r* equals **testing**. A broom without the *b* equals **room**.

Page 17

The message on the blackboard tells Frank the code which opens the door to the Testing Room. The letters of the message actually form four chemical symbols seen earlier in the book.

He = Helium
Li = Lithium
P = Phosphorous
Me = Mercury

The symbol for Lithium can be seen on the poster for batteries in the Scientists' labs (page 4). The rest of the symbols can be seen in Professor Bunsen's laboratory on page 15.

Frank spots Professor Slick's cunning clue and presses the four buttons in the right order to open the door.

Pages 18-19

Ken has solved the flask task by finding the only acid in the room. Litmus paper is used to test whether a substance is an acid or an alkali. Blue litmus paper turns pink when in contact with an acid. Pink litmus paper turns blue when in contact with an alkali.

The liquid that Ken had accidentally dripped onto the litmus paper has turned it pink, showing that the flask in Ken's hand is an acid.

Pages 20-21

If you look carefully, on the left-hand side of page 20, you can see that Rosie has slipped the label off the bottle containing the friction restorer. The label has the chemical formula of the friction restorer written on it. The chemical formula tells a chemist precisely what a substance is made from. This would help Suki back at the Mad Scientists' Laboratories.

Pages 22-23

When Dr. Genius says "I **bet** you can," to Frank, he's dropping a hint about the bet at the start of the adventure. Blowing between the two balls caused them to move toward each other. Blowing between the two wire connectors here in Max Chaos's factory will produce exactly the same result.

LOWER AIR PRESSURE

Blowing causes the air between the connectors to move faster, but with less air pressure. The air on the outer sides of the connectors presses harder than the air between the two connectors. The difference in pressure forces the wire connectors toward each other so that they touch.

HIGHER AIR PRESSURE

Pages 24-25

Elton uses his coat to smother the fire. Three essential ingredients are needed to make something burn: fuel, oxygen and heat. These are shown in the fire triangle.

Firefighters put out fires by removing at least one of these three things. For example, fire breaks (a corridor cleared of trees) are used, when fighting forest fires, to cut off the fire's supply of fuel.

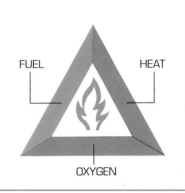

FUEL   HEAT

OXYGEN

Pages 26-27
The safe route through the maze is marked in black.

Pages 28-29
The thermometer works by showing Suki the temperature at which the water samples boil. The sample that boils at exactly 100°C is pure. A substance is pure if it contains no trace of any other substance. Pure substances have fixed boiling points and pure water's boiling point is 100°C.

Pages 30-31
Rosie was waiting for some blue ink to be drawn up the stem of a white carnation to turn the flower's petals blue. This takes a number of hours and is an example of capillary action.

Capillary action is the way that fluids travel up narrow tubes. Plants draw water up from their roots, through their stems and into their leaves and flowers.

You can try the experiment with different flowers. Food dye works even faster than ink.

Did you notice a poster showing capillary action at work in the Mad Scientist's laboratory on page 5?

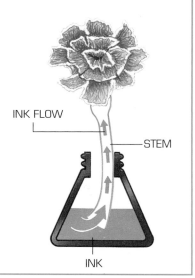

INK FLOW

STEM

INK

Pages 32-33
The waiter is disgraced goalkeeper, Gordon Gloves. You can find a picture of him on the newspaper on page 11.

Pages 34-35
The plump figure is Dr. Genius. You can see the snorkel sticking out of his suitcase on page 29.

Pages 36-37

Dr. Genius spotted the car under covers at Max Chaos's factory on page 26. On page 10, Simone Slick explained how all brakes need friction to work. Dr. Genius believes that Max Chaos has coated the brake pads with the antifriction liquid.

When the brake pedal is pressed, the brake pads are pushed firmly onto part of the car's wheels. The pads touching the wheels create a very large amount of friction, which slows down the wheels.

BRAKE PADS

Pages 38-39

The parachute will create a large amount of friction with the air. This extra friction will slow down Professor Slick's sports car, just as it would work on Elton's dragster, or on the aircraft shown in Professor Slick's office on page 10.

Pages 40-41

Because Professor Slick's car is acting as a balance. The underside of the car caught on the cliff edge is the balancing point. The front of the car and the back of the car are balancing each other out.

If the passengers in the back leave the car, the balance of the car will shift, the front end will be heavier than the back, and the car will plunge over the cliff. Dr. Genius cleverly realizes that Simone Slick and Frank must get out of the front of the car first. This changes the balance making the back of the car heavier than the front, which keeps it on the cliff edge.

EQUAL WEIGHT IN FRONT AND REAR

WEIGHT IN FRONT

WEIGHT IN REAR

First published in 1996 by Usborne Publishing Ltd, Usborne House, 83-85 Saffron Hill, London EC1N 8RT, England. Copyright © 1996 Usborne Publishing Ltd.

The name Usborne and the device 🪂 are Trade Marks of Usborne Publishing Ltd. All rights reserved.

Printed in Great Britain   UE
First published in America, August 1996.